T5-CVG-983

The Man from Mars

by Pat Edwards

Illustrated by Richard Mitchell

sundance

Simon

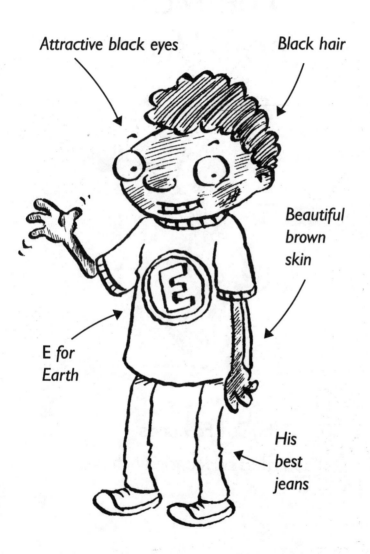

Attractive black eyes

Black hair

Beautiful brown skin

E for Earth

His best jeans

The man from Mars

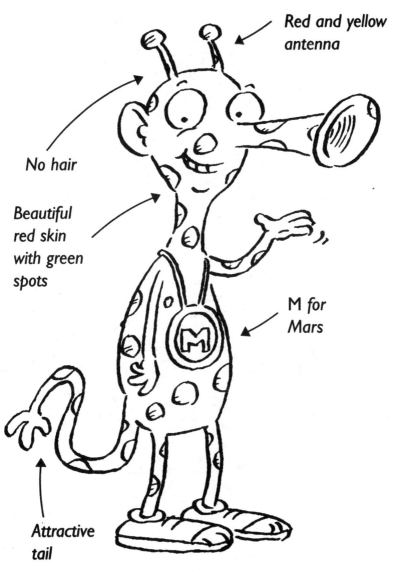

Red and yellow antenna

No hair

Beautiful red skin with green spots

M for Mars

Attractive tail

The spaceship

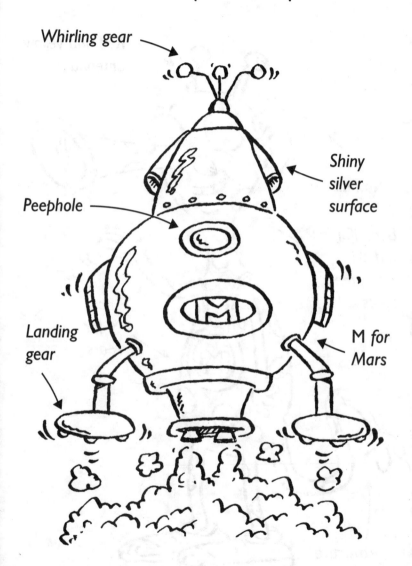

Whirling gear

Shiny silver surface

Peephole

Landing gear

M for Mars

Contents

CHAPTER 1

The Man from Mars

"It's time to get ready for the Book Week parade," said the teacher.

But Simon was looking out the window. He had just seen a spaceship landing in the playground.

"Hey, look, a spaceship," he said.

No one took any notice. They were too busy getting dressed up in their costumes. Even the teacher was too busy to listen.

Something small and strange got out of the spaceship. It looked just like the man from Mars in Simon's space book at home.

"Look, it's a man from Mars," he said.

Still no one took any notice.

"Hurry up, Simon. Put on your costume," said the teacher. "We don't have all day."

"I saw a spaceship land in the playground," said Simon loudly. "And a man from Mars got out."

"Don't be silly, Simon," said the teacher. "It's someone dressed up. The big children are coming to the parade, too. Put on your costume before I get cross."

Simon pulled on his clown costume.

"Hurry up," said the teacher. "I don't want my class to be last. Line up, now. It's time to go."

Simon looked over at the window.
The strange little man was
watching them through the glass.

"Look, it's the man from Mars,"
he said.

"Don't be silly, Simon," said the
teacher. "Come along, children,
and NO TALKING!"

CHAPTER 2
Keep in Line

They went out into the playground.
All the other classes were there and
everyone was dressed up. There
were witches and ghosts and
rabbits and Goldilocks and the
Three Bears and Superman and
the Three Little Pigs.

Simon noticed that there were other clowns, too, but he thought that his clown costume was the best. Nobody had a hat like his.

Simon saw the man from Mars. He was watching all the children line up.

"Keep in line," said the principal, pushing the man from Mars in behind Simon.

"He's real," said Simon to the principal. "He came in a spaceship."

"Don't be silly, Simon," said the principal.

Music began to play over the loudspeaker.

"Start walking," said a teacher, and they all walked around and around and around while the principal and the teachers looked at them.

Then the principal picked out one boy or girl from each class. She picked the man from Mars from Simon's class.

"That's not fair," said Simon. "He's real."

"Don't be silly, Simon," said his teacher.

Everyone sat down and watched
while the children who had been
picked walked around and around
and around to the music.

Most of the other children got tired of looking and started playing. The ghosts were trying to scare people and the clowns were trying to see who could turn the best somersaults and one of the bears made a little pig cry.

But Simon didn't want to play. He was watching the man from Mars and waiting.

CHAPTER 3

First Prize

When the music stopped, the man from Mars looked around as if he was surprised.

"I wonder what he will do?" Simon thought.

Then the principal told everyone to stop playing and sit down and listen to her.

She said all the children who had
been picked out would get a book.

"And the prize for the best
costume," she said, "goes to the
man from Mars."

All the teachers clapped and some of the children did.

"Come and get your prize," said the principal.

"That's not fair," said Simon. "He's real."

"Don't be silly, Simon," said his teacher. She went over to the man from Mars.

"Go on, dear," she said to him.

But the man from Mars took no notice. He didn't move. The teacher looked at him.

"I don't know who you are," she said. "Let's take off your costume, dear."

The man from Mars jumped away from her. Then he turned and ran across the playground to his ship. Some of the children ran after him.

"Look," they shouted. "It's a spaceship!"

"I told you there was a spaceship," said Simon. "I told you he was real."

The spaceship took off.

"Wow! Look at it go!" everyone shouted.

"Oh, my goodness, he *was* real!" said Simon's teacher.

"I told you he was," said Simon.

"Now, who do we give the prize to?" asked the principal. "Don't tell me we have to do it all over again."

"You could give it to me," said Simon.

"Don't be silly," said his teacher.

CHAPTER 4

I Told Them!

The TV reporters came to the school to find out about the man from Mars.

They didn't want to talk to the principal and they didn't want to talk to any of the teachers.

They wanted to talk to Simon.

"I told them he was real," Simon
said. "I told them lots of times."

And this time EVERYONE
listened.

More Popcorn space stories
by Pat Edwards

The Monster from Mercury

When the monster from Mercury meets Jess, it immediately decides to change her.
It makes her green!

Planet X

When Joseph visits Planet X, he gets into awful trouble.
He's adopted as a pet!

Jupiter Spiders and Other Scary Creatures

When Mip and Mup visit Jupiter, they get a real surprise.
But there's a bigger one waiting back home!